Madalena Matoso

Story Path

Kane Miller
A DIVISION OF EDC PUBLISHING

How to Use Story Path

Story Path is a special kind of story — one where YOU get to choose whom you meet, where you go and what you do.

It's easy...

* just decide which path you'd like to follow
* describe what you see
* then follow the path on to the next page

Want to ride an elephant through an enchanted forest, battle a troll or dress up like a princess? Want to meet a spooky cat, or turn a hairy monster into a teapot? Anything is possible with Story Path!

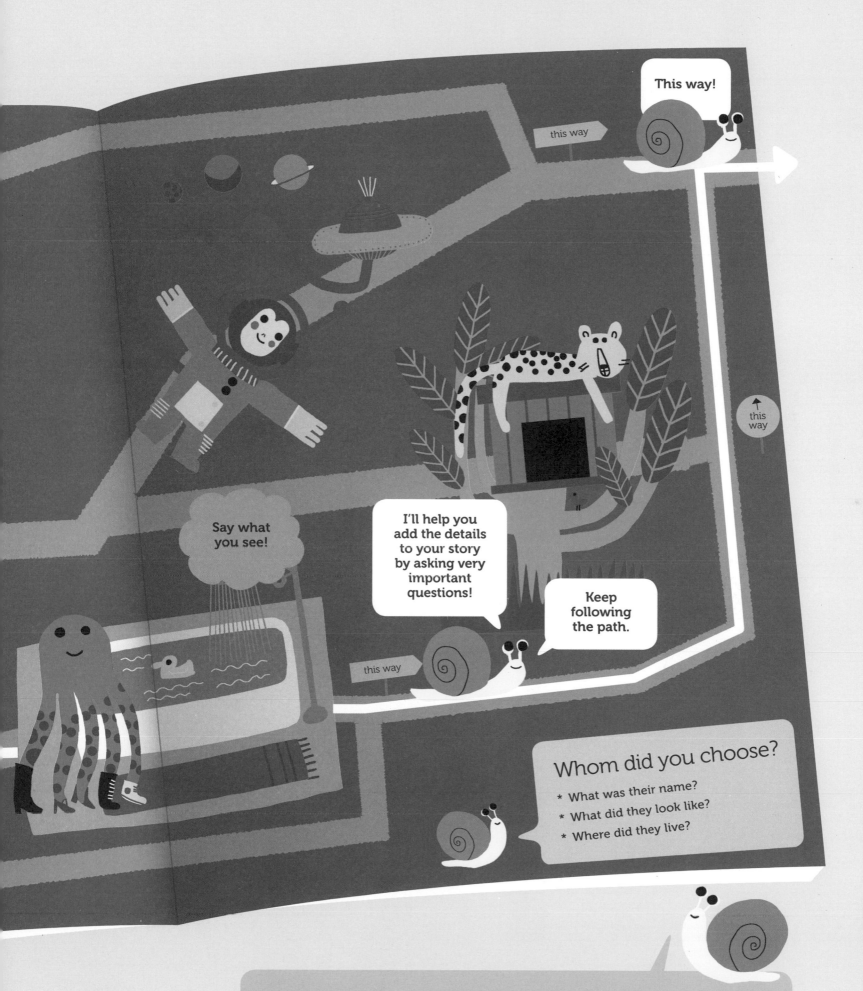

Are you ready? Then turn the page...

...and let's begin!

Once upon a time

there lived a...

this way

this way

this way

this way

Whom did you choose?

* What was their name?
* What did they look like?
* Where did they live?

One day,
they were riding
along on their...

As they turned the corner they were stopped by a mysterious...

this way

who gave them a magical...

What did they choose?

this way

They reached out to touch it...

↑ this way

Whom did you choose?

* Can you describe them?
* What did they say?
* Were they friendly?

this way

this way

What did you choose?

* What did it look like?
* What did it smell like?
* Who else was there?

They followed the path this way and that until they came across a...

KEEP OFF THE SAND

this way

WELCOME

this way

What did you choose?

* How big was it?
* Did it look cozy?
* Who do you think lived there?

They
knocked
on the
door
and it was
opened by
a family of
friendly...

this way

this way

They invited them in for a tasty meal of...

What did they eat?

Whom did you choose?

* Can you describe them?
* What did they all talk about?
* What was it like inside their house?

Suddenly, there was a crash of thunder! Standing in the doorway was a mean and scary...

They were trapped!
But then they spied
an enchanted...

which turned the
monster into a...

As they made their escape,

they discovered a room full of clothes. They quickly disguised themselves as a...

this way

Then they put on a...

Which one did they choose?

this way

What did you choose?

* What color was the outfit?
* Did it fit?
* Did anyone see them?

They crept into the next room where they stumbled upon a...

this way

this way

Which one did you choose?

* How heavy was it?
* What was inside?
* What was the best treasure?

With their pockets full of treasure they ran outside, where they found a...

this way

this way

this way

What did you choose?

* How big was it?
* What was it made of?
* Did it make a noise?

They sped
off as fast
as lightning.
Along the way
they saw...

Finally, they made it home.

They told their friends all about their adventure and then they...

before falling asleep in their...

this way

this way

What did you choose?

* Was it comfy?

* How long did they sleep for?

* What did they dream about?

...and they lived happily ever after.

The
End

To be continued...

Kane Miller, A Division of EDC Publishing

First published in the UK in 2016 by Big Picture Press,
part of the Bonnier Publishing Group

Illustration copyright © 2016 by Madalena Matoso
Text and design copyright © 2016 by The Templar Company Limited
Concept and design by Kim Hankinson
Written and edited by Kate Baker

For information contact:
Kane Miller, A Division of EDC Publishing
PO Box 470663
Tulsa, OK 74147-0663
www.kanemiller.com
www.edcpub.com
www.usbornebooksandmore.com

Library of Congress Control Number: 2016941595

Printed in China

2 3 4 5 6 7 8 9 10

ISBN: 978-1-61067-604-5